NL

Bat and Sloth Throw a Party

Time to Read® is an early reader program designed to guide children to literacy success regardless of age or grade level. The program's three levels correspond to stages of reading readiness, making book selection straightforward, and assuring that when it's time for a child to read, the right book is waiting.

Beginning to Read

- Large, simple type
- Basic vocabulary
- Word repetition
- Strong illustration support

Reading with Help

- Short sentences
- Engaging stories
- Simple dialogue
- Illustration support

Reading Independently

- Longer sentences
- Harder words
- Short paragraphs
- Increased story complexity

To my mother, whose parties have always been the best—LK

To Rose and Aliyah—SB

Library of Congress Cataloging-in-Publication data
is on file with the publisher.

Illustrations by Seb Braun
First published in the United States of America in 2021
by Albert Whitman & Company
ISBN 978-0-8075-0581-6 (hardcover)
ISBN 978-0-8075-0577-9 (ebook)

Printed in China
10 9 8 7 6 5 4 3 2 1 RRD 24 23 22 21 20

Design by Valerie Hernández

For more information about Albert Whitman & Company,
visit our website at www.albertwhitman.com.

Bat and Sloth Throw a Party

Leslie Kimmelman

illustrated by
Seb Braun

Albert Whitman & Company
Chicago, Illinois

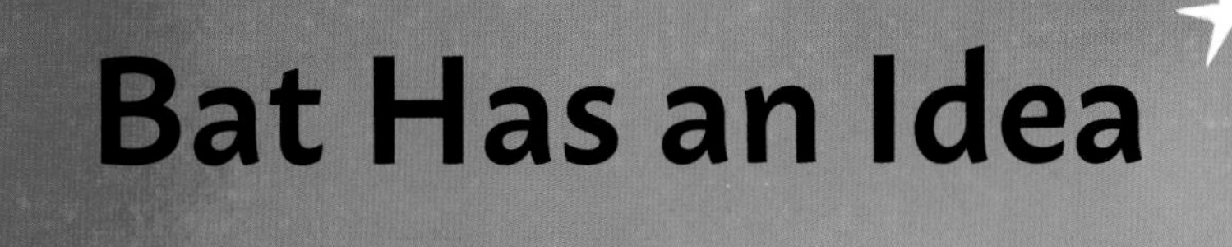

Bat Has an Idea

Deep in the rain forest,
late at night,
Bat and Sloth were talking.

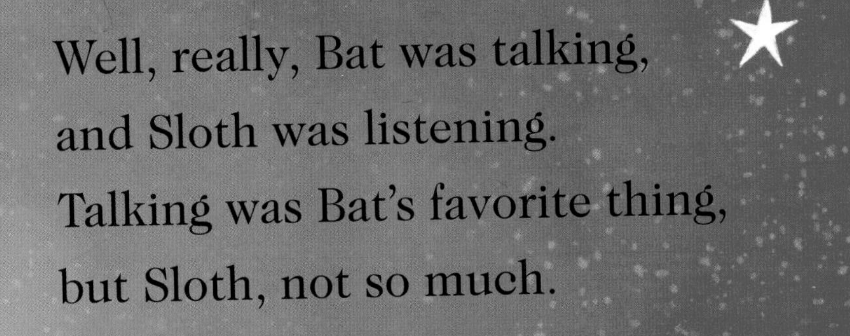

Well, really, Bat was talking,
and Sloth was listening.
Talking was Bat's favorite thing,
but Sloth, not so much.

“We have lots of friends, right?”
Bat asked Sloth.
“Yes,” Sloth agreed.
“We have a nice home, right?”
Bat asked Sloth.
“Yes,” Sloth agreed.

"Then we should have a party!" said Bat.

"Um," Sloth began.

Parties tired Sloth out.

But Bat was too excited to listen.

He zipped off the branch.

He zapped around the trunk.

Sloth was sleepy.

He did not zip or zap.

He yawned.

Bat returned to the branch.
"Now," he asked Sloth,
"what kind of party should we have?"
"I know!" he answered himself.
"We can have a surprise party!"
"How can it be a surprise,"
said Sloth, "if we both know about it?"

"You are right," said Bat.
"Maybe a costume party?"
"I feel silly in a costume," said Sloth.
He yawned again.
"Parties are hard work," said Bat.
Sloth fell asleep. *ZZAahhchhhzzz.*
"Great idea, Sloth!" said Bat.
"A sleepover party!"
And he fell asleep too.

Party Planning

"Who should come to our party?"
Bat asked the next night.
"Are you sure you want a party?"
said Sloth.
He was tired just thinking about it.
"It will be fun," said Bat.
"We can invite Kinkajou and Toucan."

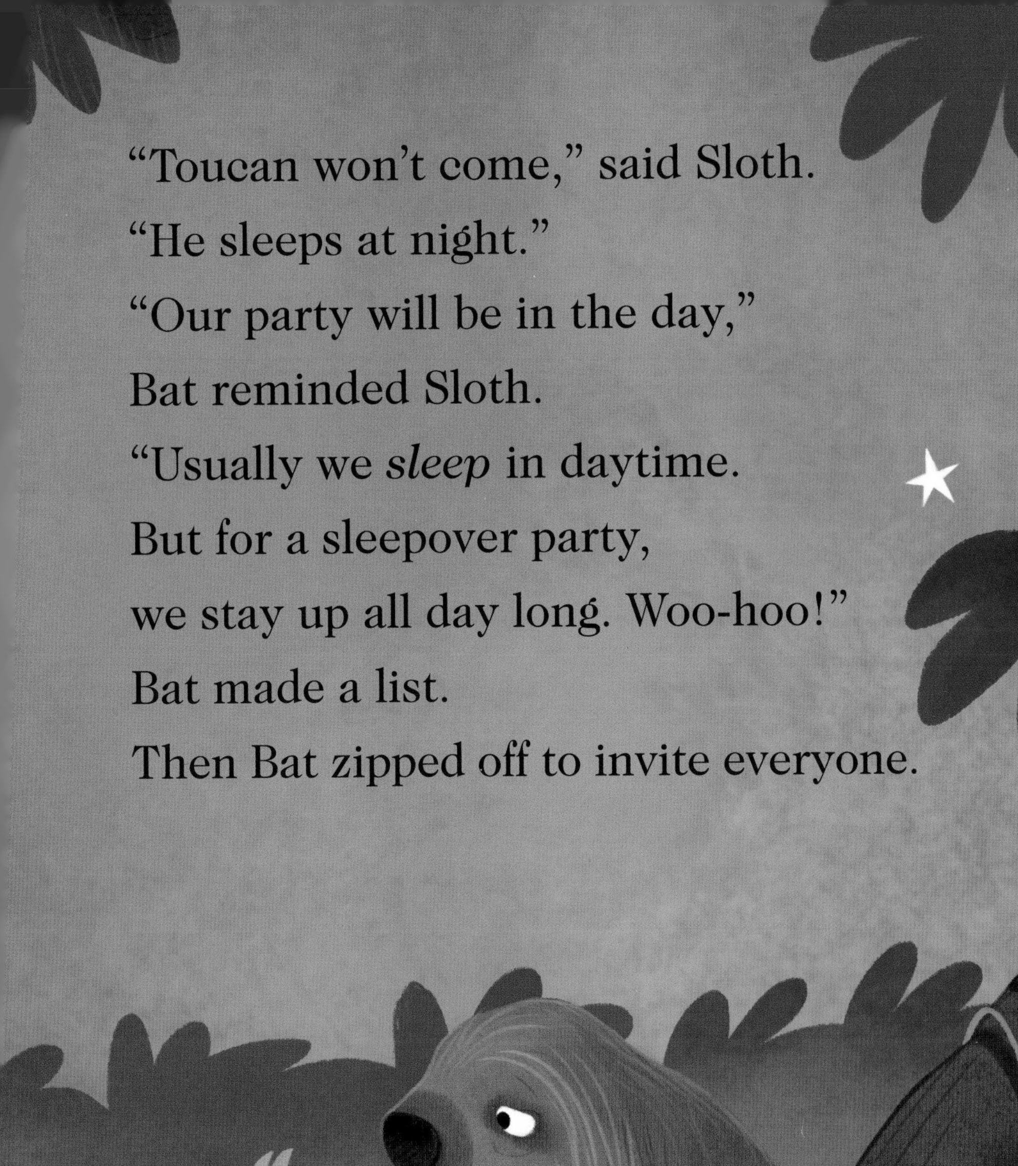

"Toucan won't come," said Sloth.
"He sleeps at night."
"Our party will be in the day,"
Bat reminded Sloth.
"Usually we *sleep* in daytime.
But for a sleepover party,
we stay up all day long. Woo-hoo!"
Bat made a list.
Then Bat zipped off to invite everyone.

"Kinkajou, Toucan, Iguana, and Agouti
are all coming!"
Bat said when he returned.
"Now what can we have for party food?"
"We need food too?" asked Sloth.

"Lots of fruit," said Bat, not listening.
"I am a fruit bat after all."
The party was tomorrow.
So Bat flew off to gather the fruit.

“Banango cake,” Bat said when he returned,
“is an old family recipe.”
“One banana for me,” he said,
“one for you, Sloth.
And one for the cake.”

“One mango for me,” Bat said,
“one for you, Sloth.” He paused.
“And one for the cake.”
They mashed and mixed.
They stirred, poured, and tasted.
Then they put the cake in the sun to
bake and went to sleep.

When the two friends woke up,
the moon was rising,
and it was raining.
“Oh no!” said Bat.
“Our party will be ruined.”

“Silly,” said Sloth.
“It’s a rain forest.
It’s *supposed* to rain.”
“Right,” said Bat. “I forgot.
“But won’t our cake be ruined?”
“Do not worry,” said Sloth.

Party!

The rain stopped just before sunrise.

The guests arrived right on time.

All day long, animals flew, swung, and swam

“See?” said Bat. “Parties are fun!”
Sloth had to admit Bat was right.
It was so much fun that
he almost forgot to be sleepy.
Almost.

“I am going to tell a ghost story!”
Kinkajou announced.
The animals gathered around.
“Once upon a time,
there was a BIG GHOST SNAKE.”
“Who’s afraid of snakes?” scoffed Bat.
“You are, Bat,” Sloth reminded him.
“Snakes scare you silly!”
Kinkajou went on with the story.

“It was an EXTREMELY dangerous ghost snake.”

“Bah!” said Bat, trembling. “That doesn’t scare me.”

“You could almost see through it,” said Kinkajou. “That snake was hard to spot.”

“It wouldn’t trick *me*,” said Bat. “I am much too smart.”

Kinkajou went on with the story.
"The snake slithered along the ground.
Gulp! It ate a lizard."
Iguana shivered.

“It slunk around tree trunks.
Gulp! It ate an agouti.”
Agouti quivered.
“Don’t worry,” Bat told his friends.
“It is just a story.”

Kinkajou continued.
"Slowly, sssslowly,
it sssssssnuck along a tree branch."
Bat was hanging from a tree branch.
"HELP! HELP!" he shouted suddenly.
Something long and thin was wrapped
around him.

“Do not worry, Bat,” said Kinkajou.
“That is just my tail.
There is no such thing as a ghost snake.”
“I knew that,” said Bat in a shaky voice.
“Now who would like some cake?”

Fast Asleep

"You were right," said Sloth later.
"Your sleepover party was fun! But
I am very tired."
"For the first time, I think that
I am even more tired than you,"
said Bat.
He checked for snakes.

Then he said,
"I will sing you to sleep
with a song I made up.

With our friends or eating cake,
fast asleep or wide awake,
for Sloth and me, the place to be
is hanging on our favorite tree."

The moon was rising.
In the cool of the night,
two best friends hung upside down
from their branch, on their tree,
deep in the rain forest.

It was a special Bat and Sloth
sleep-UNDER party.

Bat's Upside-Down Banango Cake

Ingredients

1 ripe mango
1 large banana
2 Tbsp fresh lemon juice
1 Tbsp unsalted butter
⅓ cup dark brown sugar, packed
¼ cup unsalted butter
⅔ cup sugar
¼ cup plain yogurt
1 large egg
1 tsp vanilla
½ cup milk
1 ¼ cups flour
2 tsp baking powder
⅛ tsp salt

Directions

1. Slice the mango, and put the slices into a small bowl. Pour lemon juice over the mango, and let stand for 10–15 minutes. Preheat oven to 350°F.
2. Melt 1 Tbsp butter in an 8-inch round cake pan. Lightly sprinkle brown sugar over melted butter. Set aside a few mango slices, then arrange the rest over the brown sugar. Slice half of the banana, and arrange the banana slices with the mango slices in the pan.
3. In a large bowl, cream the butter. Add sugar, yogurt, egg, vanilla, and the remaining ½ banana, mashed.
4. In a small bowl, combine the flour, baking powder, and salt together; add to the butter mixture alternately with the milk, and stir until smooth. Pour batter into the pan over the fruit.
5. Bake for 50–60 minutes, until golden brown on top. Let the cake rest for 15 minutes, then run a knife around the sides and turn upside down on a plate to serve.